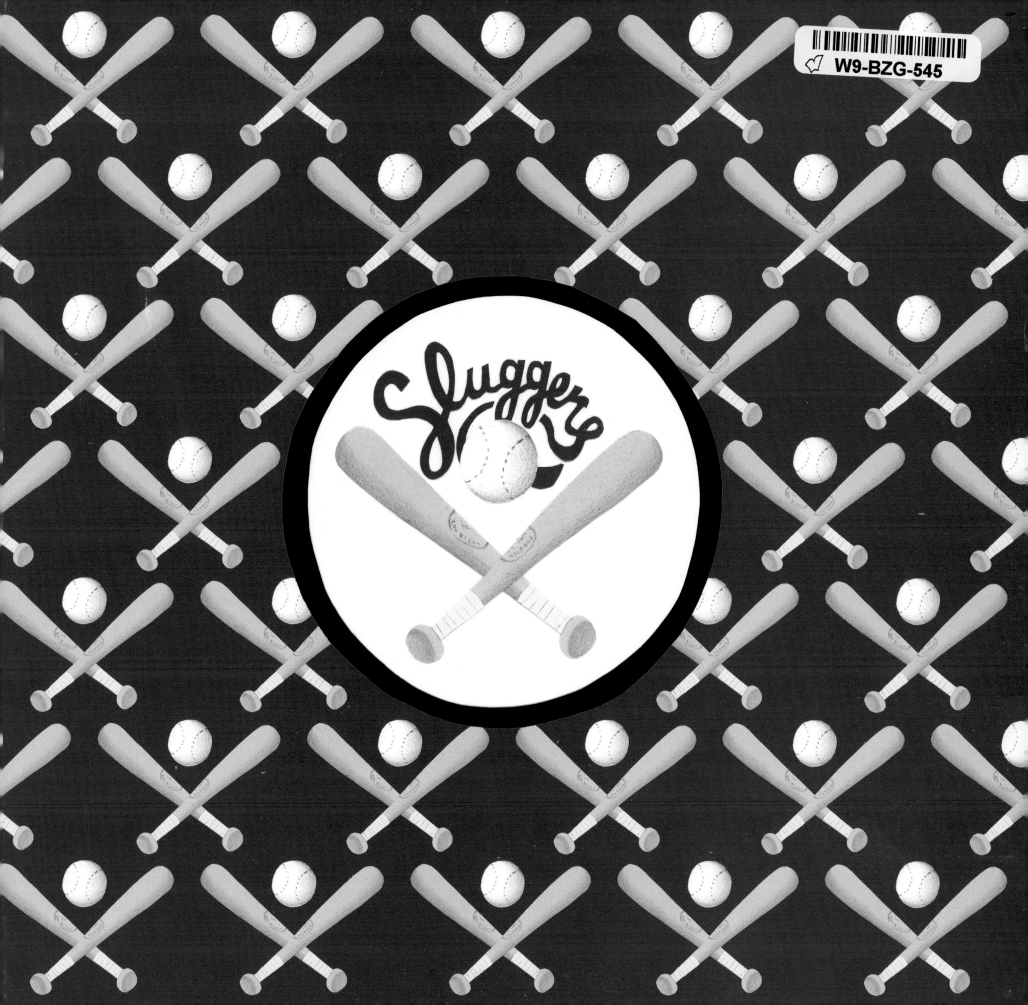

Take Me Out to the Ball Game

PERFORMED BY **Carly Simon**

ILLUSTRATED BY **Amiko Hirao**

WRITTEN BY **Jack Norworth**

imagine!
a Peter Yarrow Book

Katie Casey was baseball mad.
She had the fever and she had it bad.
Just to root for the hometown crew,
every cent, that Katie spent.

On one Saturday her young beau
called to see if she'd like to go
to see a show, but Ms. Kate said "No,
I'll tell you what you can do."

Take me out to the ball game,
take me out with the crowd.
Buy me some peanuts and Cracker Jacks.
I don't care if I ever get back.

HOT DOGS

SLUGGERS

'Cause it's root, root, root for the home team,
if they don't win, it's a shame.
'Cause it's

ONE, TWO, THREE

strikes, you're out,
at the old ball game.

Katie Casey saw all the games,
knew all the players by their first names.
Told the umpire he was wrong,
all along, and she was strong.

When the score was 2–2,
Katie Casey, she had the clue,
to cheer on the boys,
she knew just what to do.

She made everyone sing this song:

Take me out to the ball game,
take me out with the crowd.
Buy me some peanuts and Cracker Jacks.
I do not care if I ever get back.

GGERS
1 2 3 4 5 6 7 8 9 10
2
2
BALL STRIKE OUT
H
PEAN
SLUGGERS
ROGO
DRINKS

'Cause it's root, root, root for the home team,
if they don't win, it's a shame.

SLUGGERS
1 2 3 4 5
DIAMONDS 0 0 0 0 1
SLUGGERS 0 0 1 0 0

AT BAT   BALL   STRIK

COTTON
CANDY

'Cause it's ONE, TWO, THREE
strikes, you're out,
at the old ball game.

Take me out to the ball game,
take me out with the crowd.
Buy me some peanuts and Cracker Jacks.
I don't care if I ever get back.

'Cause it's root, root, root for the home team,
if they don't win, it's a shame.

Performer's Note

No one will believe me when I tell you this: Jackie Robinson, that most excellent, fun, funny, and graceful gentleman, lived with my family for close to two years. This was in Stamford, Connecticut in 1954 and 1955. Stamford at that time was not integrated, and it was difficult for them to buy land and build a house. My parents went on a campaign to get those most archaic rules changed, and while all this activity was taking place, the Robinsons, all five of them, lived with us down the road from where their house was finally under construction.

I got to go to all the home games with Jackie, riding in his car to Ebbets Field. I became such a familiar sight that some of the Dodgers called me the little girl, and said that I was their "mascot."

Naturally, I was in love with baseball, though it was mostly the Brooklyn Dodgers.

When Ken Burns asked me to sing "Take Me Out to the Ball Game" for his brilliant PBS special, he didn't know I had this special connection with one of the most famous and fabulous players of all time: Jackie Robinson. Ken and I became fast friends, and getting to sing this song was, and is, so very personal. What a fine song it turned out to be, every bit of it! Katie Casey—I wonder what she was like, beyond the "fever" which she, like me, had roused in her by the song and by its very excitement.

Artist's Note

I have always loved the way, in baseball cards, the world is always sunny and the grass is always green. I wanted to make that world come alive in this book, like stepping right onto the baseball field captured in those cards. I thought that would be something Katie Casey would have enjoyed. This book is for the Katie in all of us.

Library of Congress Cataloging-in-Publication Data
Norworth, Jack.
Take me out to the ball game / performed by Carly Simon ; written by Jack
Norworth ; illustrated by Amiko Hirao.
p. cm.
Summary: Text and illustrations present the well-known song about baseball games.
ISBN 978-1-936140-26-8 (reinforced for library use)
1. Children's songs, English--United States--Texts. [1. Baseball--Songs
and music. 2. Songs.] I. Simon, Carly. II. Hirao, Amiko, ill. III. Title.
PZ8.3.N8183Tad 2011
782.42--dc22
[E]
2010035438

1 3 5 7 9 10 8 6 4 2

An Imagine Book
Published by Charlesbridge
85 Main Street
Watertown, MA 02472
617-926-0329
www.charlesbridge.com

Printed in China
Manufactured in December, 2010
Designed by Marc Cheshire

ISBN 13: 978-1-936140-26-8

For information about custom editions, special sales, premium and corporate purchases,
please contact Charlesbridge Publishing, Inc. at specialsales@charlesbridge.com